Woodland Fairies
Helping and Having Fun

written by Nayera Salam
illustrated by Natasha Wescoat

Author of
1. Go Away Bad Mood
Illustrated by Elsa Estrada
2. Big Elephant Fritz and the Tiny Ants
Illustrated by Bina Damodar
3. A Cat and Mouse Pact
Illustrated by Teresa Abboud

Natasha Wescoat is a whimsical artist. Through this fanciful, playful style of art, she brings life to the characters with her enigmatic mix of colors. Whimsical art, sometimes labelled as erratic, uses eccentric expression to show surreal, imaginative characters such as fairies, elves, trolls, and monsters. Natasha's art is vibrant and quirky. Whimsical art is known to be carefree and fun.

PROLANCE

Prolance

www.prolancewriting.com
California, USA
©2018 Nayera Salam
Illustrations ©2018 Natasha Wescoat

ISBN: 978-0-9996991-0-2

To Yasmine
with love

We look after every plant and every flower,
Every day, hour after hour!
We play music, we sing, we dance, and we have fun,
And we help our woodland friends, one by one.

We have special potions,
Extraordinary lotions,
And a magic cream
To soothe and heal
A swollen ankle, or a sore knee.

A bad cough, Mr. McHowell?
Don't you worry, gentle owl,
A few sips of our fairy brew,
And you'll be good as new.

Sweet Suzette, are you lost?
You're scared and tired!
We'll take you back to your warm nest,
Where you can sleep and have some rest.

Lady Lala, Lady Lala, don't sob, don't cry,
Your spots are fading and you don't know why.
Calm down, pretty lady, relax and wait!
In a minute we'll be back, we won't be late.
We'll bring our brushes and some black and red paint!

We're Jasmine, Rosie and Bluebell,
Call us, we'll hear you, and we'll come!
We'll play music, we'll dance, we'll sing, we'll have fun,
And we'll help our woodland friends, one by one.

Nayera Salam

"Mommy, Daddy, look!" said Linh.

"My wish came true. The woodland fairies are there, under the weeping willow."

Linh ran down the hill from the cottage to the weeping willow by the pond.

"Happy birthday, Linh. We heard your wish and here we are," whispered the woodland fairies.

"I am *Jasmine*."

"I am **Rosie**."

"I am Bluebell."

Bluebell played the violin, while Jasmine and Rosie danced a joyful dance and sang a merry song.

"Thank you, Linh, for the house you built just for us. Thank you for the marshmallows, milk, and blueberries.

Thank you for looking after the bushes, the vines, the flowers, and the trees.

We'll now celebrate your day in our special fairy way."

Linh, Jasmine, Rosie, and Bluebell played hide and seek with Flutter, Papillon, and Beautyfly.

They collected wild flowers, pine cones, acorns, and hazelnuts with Nibbler, Chipper, and Bushytail. They skipped around with Grassy, Hopper, and Woody Greenvest.

Then it was time for a picnic with the Velvet Ears.

Linh, Jasmine, Rosie, and Bluebell sat on the soft grass and had a yummy snack with Papa Buttons, Biscuit, Bella, Mama Cinnamon Bun, and Baby Bubblegum.

They ate carrots, raspberries, and fresh lettuce leaves.

What a treat!

"I'm ready for a nap," said Jasmine as she flapped her wings.

"Not yet, Jasmine, Mrs. Ribbitson is waiting for us by the pond," said Bluebell.

"I love her funny tales about her wiggly tadpoles, Flipper, Frisky, Frogricka, and Froguette, with their long, flat tails."

"Oh dear! We have to leave. I hear someone crying, not too far from here," whispered Jasmine in Linh's ear." It's Little Suzette. She's lost and needs help. We must find Mama Coquette. She'll take her back to the nest."

"Cheep cheep," chirped Mama Coquette. "You're very kind. I missed my sweet Suzette, and I almost lost my mind!"

"Now we can have some rest," said Jasmine and Bluebell.

"Rest? Did you forget? We need to check on old Uncle McBuck. He fell and hurt his knees last night," said Rosie.

"You're in luck, dear Uncle McBuck," said Linh, Jasmine, Rosie, and Bluebell as they examined his knees and rubbed them with some peppermint cream.

"It was a bad fall, but no broken bones. By tomorrow you won't be sore, and your knees will hurt no more."

Linh and her friends were heading back to the weeping willow by the pond, when Bluebell saw Lady Lala sobbing on a rosebud .

"My spots are dull and my beauty is gone. There's nothing left!" she whined and wept.

Linh, Jasmine, Rosie, and Bluebell listened to Lady Lala's complaint and quickly got their brushes and red and black paint.

Now bright and jolly, Lady Lala smiled a happy ladybug smile, gave Linh and the fairies a happy ladybug hug, and cheerfully crawled away.

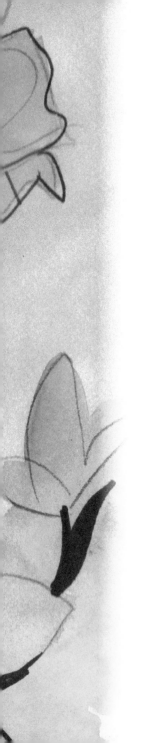

It was getting late, but Grandma Ollie was wide awake, and her loud hoot-hoot-hoot filled the air.

"It's Grandpa Howell," she screeched. "He coughed, sneezed, and wheezed all night. I know something isn't right."

Jasmine, Rosie, Bluebell, and Linh rushed to her side. They prepared a soothing fairy brew of coconut milk, blackberry seeds, lemon peel, maple syrup, and honeydew.

"Don't you worry," they told Grandma Ollie. "It's a nasty cold, but it isn't the flu. In a day or two, Grandpa Howell will be as good as new."

The day slowly came to an end. The fairies walked with Linh all the way to the cottage, waved goodbye, fluttered their wings, and disappeared.

Almost every day, all summer long, Linh joined her fairy friends under the weeping willow by the pond. They drank cranberry tea from acorn shell cups and ate raisins, sugar cookies, and nuts. They sang, played and danced, and they always looked after the woodland animals and plants.

"This story is great! It was funny! I liked the names of the fairies and birds...I want to hear it again and again..."
--Theo, Age 5
New York

About the Author:
Nayera Salam has a Master's degree in Education from Emory University, Atlanta, Georgia, and more than thirty years teaching experience. She is now retired and lives in Atlanta with her husband. She has two children and is the proud grandmother of two granddaughters.

About the Illustrator:
Natasha Wescoat is a professional artist-entrepreneur with 12+ years of experience. She has become a household name with over 1000 original works in private and corporate collections worldwide. She has nabbed over 20 licensing deals, several nationwide art exhibits and has even had her art in major publications and Hollywood films.

CPSIA information can be obtained
at www.ICGtesting.com
Printed in the USA
LVHW071207060219
606258LV00006B/20/P